Adapted by Lisa Ann Marsoli
Based on the episode written by Ashley Mendoza
Illustrated by Loter, Inc.

DISNEP PRESS

New York • Los Angeles

Copyright © 2014 Disney Enterprises, Inc. All rights reserved. Published by Disney Press, an imprint of Disney Book Group. No part of this book may be reproduced or transmitted in any form or by any means, electronic or mechanical, including photocopying, recording, or by any information storage and retrieval system, without written permission from the publisher. For information address Disney Press, 1101 Flower Street, Glendale, California 91201.

First Edition 10 9 8 7 6 5 4 3 2 1
ISBN 978-1-4231-6417-3
J689-1817-1-13333

Manufactured in the USA
For more Disney Press fun, visit www.disneybooks.com

Mickey wants to surprise Minnie.
He needs to keep Minnie busy.
"Can you take care of my frog?"
Goofy asks.

"And sweep the floor?" Daisy adds.
"And wash my rubber duckies?"
says Donald.

"I have a lot to do," says Minnie.
First she washes the rubber duckies.

Next she fixes Pluto's bear.
"I'm so tired," says Minnie.
 Soon she is asleep!

"Minnie-rella!" a voice calls.
"I'm your fairy godmother! It's time
to get ready for Prince Mickey's ball!"
Minnie-rella has too much to do.

The Fairy Godmother will help.
She waves her wand.
Oops! Flowers grow out of the floor!
"Oh, Quoodles," she calls.

Quoodles brings a pillow, a hippo,
a ribbon, and the mystery tool.
They will save the tools for later.

The Handy Helpers help clean.
"Now you can go to Prince Mickey's ball,"
the Fairy Godmother says.

"I need a dress," says Minnie-rella.
"Here," the Fairy Godmother says.
Oh, no! The dress is in pieces!
"Oops!" says the Fairy Godmother.

The Fairy Godmother whistles.
Some little friends come to help.
Soon Minnie-rella has a lovely dress.

Now Minnie-rella needs a new bow.
"Hmmm," says the Fairy Godmother.
"Which tool can we use?"
"The ribbon!" says Minnie-rella.

The Fairy Godmother looks down.
"Your shoes won't do at all!" she cries.

She waves her
wand once.

"Oops!"

She tries again.

"Oops!"

"Once more," says
the Fairy Godmother.

"That's it!"

"You're ready!" says the Fairy Godmother.
"How will I get there?" asks Minnie-rella.
They go to Goofy's garden.

The Fairy Godmother asks for a pumpkin.
"I don't have any pumpkins," Goofy says.
"But I've got a big tomato."

The tomato turns into a carriage.
Goofy turns into a coachman!
"Be home before midnight!"
says the Fairy Godmother.

On the way to the ball, the carriage
gets stuck in a hole!
Minnie-rella calls Quoodles.
Which tool can help?

Maybe the hippo can push the
carriage out of the hole!
The hippo taps the carriage.
Away it goes!

Soon Minnie-rella and Goofy come
to the castle gate.
"It takes three diamonds to unlock
the gate," Pete says.

Quoodles brings the mystery tool.
It is a bracelet with three diamonds.
The three diamonds unlock the gate.
Minnie-rella can go to the ball!

Minnie-rella runs to the ball.
She dances with Prince Mickey.
Prince Mickey has found his princess!

Soon it is midnight.

"I have to go!" cries Minnie-rella.

"Wait! I don't know your name,"
Prince Mickey calls.

"How will I find her?" he asks.
Pluto sees the glass slipper.
Prince Mickey must find the one
who fits the glass slipper.

Prince Mickey begins his search.
Goofy tries on the glass slipper.
It does not fit.

The slipper is going to break!
Quoodles brings the pillow.
Prince Mickey catches the slipper!

Goofy takes him to see Minnie-rella.
The glass slipper fits!

The prince and princess will live happily ever after!

"Wake up, Minnie!" call her friends.
Mickey gives her a present.
"I dreamed of shoes like these!"
Minnie says. "Thank you!"

"You look like a princess,"
says Mickey.
"You'll always be my prince!"
Minnie says.

The friends do the Hot Dog Dance.
Minnie loves her new glass slippers.
She does the best dance of all!